KT-199-088

the
TRAPDOOR
mysteries

THE SCENT OF DANGER

ABIE LONGSTAFF
Illustrations by James Brown

LITTLE, BROWN BOOKS FOR YOUNG READERS

First published in Great Britain in 2018 by Hodder and Stoughton

3 5 7 9 10 8 6 4 2

Text copyright © Abie Longstaff, 2018
Illustrations copyright © James Brown, 2018

The moral rights of the author and illustrator have been asserted.
All characters and events in this publication, other than those clearly
in the public domain, are fictitious and any resemblance to
real persons, living or dead, is purely coincidental.

All rights reserved.
No part of this publication may be reproduced, stored in
a retrieval system, or transmitted, in any form or by any means, without
the prior permission in writing of the publisher, nor be otherwise circulated
in any form of binding or cover other than that in which it is published
and without a similar condition including this condition being
imposed on the subsequent purchaser.

A CIP catalogue record for this book
is available from the British Library.

ISBN 978-1-5102-002-27

Printed and bound by
CPI Group (UK) Ltd, Croydon, CR0 4YY

The paper and board used in this book are
made from wood from responsible sources.

MIX
Paper from
responsible sources
FSC® C104740

Little, Brown Books for Young Readers
An imprint of
Hachette Children's Group
Part of Hodder and Stoughton
Carmelite House
50 Victoria Embankment
London EC4Y 0DZ

An Hachette UK Company
www.hachette.co.uk
www.hachettechildrens.co.uk

For Mum and Dad – who bought a house with a trapdoor and a tapestry.

– A. L.

For Jessica and Emily who love the seaside.

– J. B.

The Secret Library's Rules:

There will be only one Secret Keeper in each generation.

The Secret Keeper must be under the age of thirteen.

The Keeper must guard the secret of the library and the information within.

Talking is permitted.

CHAPTER ONE

Tally stood at the study window, cleaning the glass with a feather duster. The manor grounds looked beautiful, sparkling in the sunshine.

Mollett Manor had once been a monastery. Lots had changed since the monks had lived there hundreds of years ago, making their honey and ale. But not everything …

The beehives were still there.

The lighthouse tower was still there.

The coded passages were still there.

And so was the Secret Library, hidden beneath the ancient stone circle.

'Ah, Tally!' Lord Mollett came into the study. 'Ready for our lesson?'

Tally turned from the window. She loved learning from Lord Mollett! He was the kindest person in the whole world. Thanks to him, for one blissful hour every day, Tally got to do history and French and geography instead of polishing and cleaning and scrubbing.

Lord Mollett sat down at his desk and held out his hand. In his palm were four fresh blackberries. There was a squeak from an armchair and a furry red shape shot into the air. It was Squill, Tally's squirrel friend. He somersaulted and landed perfectly on the polished oak desk.

Lord Mollett pulled out his white silk handkerchief and draped it over the inkwell to make a little table. He set the berries neatly on a teeny doll's-house plate, with a miniature knife and fork, and even a candelabra.

'Bon appétit,[1] Squill,' he said, as Squill chose the biggest berry.

[1] 'Bon appétit' is French for 'Enjoy your meal'.

The squirrel ignored the neat table setting and leapt straight on to the hat stand. He loved that hat stand! While Lord Mollett and Tally were talking about geography or history or music, he would spin round and round on a hook until he was a blur of furry red. Now, he perched right at the top, nibbling the blackberry in his paws.

'Today we are going to learn about an amazing discovery!' said Lord Mollett as he rustled around on the desk, looking for something. 'Ah! Here it is.' He waved a magazine. 'This, Tally, is a science journal. In it is a wonderful article for my book!'

For the last few months, Lord Mollett had been busy writing his second book. His first one, THE HAIR STYLES OF POISONOUS SPIDERS: A Thorough Analysis, hadn't sold all that well, so for a while Lord Mollett had given up being an author. But since teaching Tally, he had decided to try again. The second book was called ETIQUETTE IN CANINES: Bone or Bone China?

And he was working hard on it every day.

Lord Mollett flicked through the journal. 'The article is about a man called Ivan Pavlov,' he said, stopping at the right page. 'He has discovered that dogs can be trained to anticipate their dinner.' Lord Mollett jabbed his finger on the paper. 'Every time Pavlov gave his dogs food, he rang a bell.'

Tally pictured the dogs lined up next to their food bowls. There was Pavlov, standing next to them. *Ding, ding* went the little bell in his hand.

'Whenever he rang the bell, the dogs would start drooling. So Pavlov began to ring the bell without giving them food, and he found they drooled anyway! The dogs had learned something – that the bell and the dinner were connected.'

Tally longed to look up more about that in the Secret Library. The books there were magic. They showed her all kinds of wonderful things. There was:

HOW TO FLY by Augusta Wind
UNDERWATER BREATHING by B.A. Fish
THE ART OF SLITHERING by Anna Conda

Tally had been using the library to look up lots of facts to help Lord Mollett.

'Dogs are very clever,' she said now. 'They can communicate using different types of barks.'

Lord Mollett got out his notebook as Tally spoke.

'They use high sounds like "Yip! Yip!" when they are excited and happy,' explained Tally, 'and low sounds like "Grrr!" when they are feeling aggressive.' Tally did her best to imitate dogs barking.

'By golly,' said Lord Mollett. 'How do you know that?'

Tally squirmed. She wasn't allowed to talk about the library – not even to Lord Mollett. 'I saw it in a book,' she replied eventually.

'Tally!' came a sharp voice from downstairs. It was Mrs Sneed, the housekeeper. Squill dived from the hat stand into Tally's pinafore pocket. 'Where are you, wretched girl?'

'I'm here,' Tally answered.

There was the sound of feet stamping up the stairs. 'You lazy, good for nothing, waste of—'

The housekeeper marched into the study. Her spiky head swivelled on her long neck as she surveyed the room.

'Oh!' Her wiry eyebrows leapt up at the sight of Lord Mollett. 'Er … I was just looking for my darling niece.'

Mrs Sneed liked to pretend Tally was family. It explained why a child would live at the manor with no pocket money and no bedroom. But the truth was, eight years ago, Mrs Sneed had found two-year-old Tally crying at the edge of the estate, where the cliff met the sea. She'd brought her back to the manor, made her a bed in the scullery sink, and set her to work – even though Tally could barely walk. Nowadays, not only could she walk but she could dust, and polish, and clean. In fact, Tally did nearly all the chores at the manor house.

'Ah. There you are,' said Mrs Sneed. 'Come along, my, er …' Mrs Sneed had used up all the nice words she knew. '… My little, uh, cabbage. We're very busy downstairs.'

'See you tomorrow!' Lord Mollett called after Tally as she followed the housekeeper down to the scullery. Sometimes Tally wondered whether Lord Mollett had any idea what really went on in the manor house.

As soon as they were alone, the smile dropped from Mrs Sneed's face.

'That's enough messing about,' she snapped as she led the way to the kitchen. 'It's polishing day. You'd better get on with cleaning that silver. Lady Beatrice likes to see her reflection in her spoon.'

'Yes, Mrs Sneed.' Tally already knew Sunday was polishing day – because she was the one who did it every week.

'I'll need some tea,' the housekeeper sighed, 'and some of your cherry biscuits. I'm exhausted from having to find you.'

'Sorry,' said Tally, putting the kettle on the fire.

Squill popped his head out of Tally's pinafore pocket. He checked Mrs Sneed wasn't looking, then waggled his eyebrows in a perfect imitation of the bossy housekeeper. Tally giggled behind her hand.

Tally set the silverware out on a pile of newspapers and picked up her polishing cloth. As she rubbed the forks, she furtively scanned the pages. An ad caught her eye:

COME TO COLIN'S CARRIAGE OF CURIOSITIES!

MARVEL AT THE DANCING GECKO!
GASP WHEN THE WHITE RAT SINGS!
APPLAUD THE BICYCLING BUDGIE!
ALL THIS PLUS
JUGGLING HAMSTERS, HIGH-WIRE ANTS,
BEES, ACROBATIC RABBITS AND MORE!
LOOK OUT FOR THE CARRIAGE
MOVING THROUGH YOUR VILLAGE ON
FRIDAY NIGHT.

A travelling curiosity show had come to the village. How exciting! She checked the date – this was last Wednesday's newspaper. That meant the show had been on last Friday night. She'd missed it ... not that Mrs Sneed would have let her go anyway.

She paused in her polishing, imagining a world where she was allowed out of the manor to go to a show. In her head, she stood among the crowd, watching the rabbits doing their best somersaults. Squill was with her, sharing a big bag of hot chestnuts ... *mmmmm* ...

There was a sharp tut from the armchair, bringing her back down to reality with a bump.

Tally quickly reached for the silver spoons. She shuffled the newspapers around until she found today's date.

Missing since yesterday!
Have you seen Mrs Marsh's cat?
It has blue eyes. One black ear, one white.
Likes ice cream and tummy rubs.

Poor cat. Tally shook her head.

Ting, ting! There was a high-pitched tinkle as a little golden bell rang on the wall of the scullery. Mrs Sneed's eyes narrowed. The bell was new – it had been installed just for Tally. Lady Beatrice Mollett used it to reach her 'best helper' in an emergency. Emergencies could be anything from getting her toothbrush stuck in her teeth to forgetting how to tie her shoelaces.

'I don't want you, Mrs Sneed,' Lady Beatrice would say, waving the housekeeper away. 'I only want Tally.'

Although Lady Beatrice kept Tally busy, it was

fun to be doing something other than cleaning.

'I'll be right back,' Tally reassured the housekeeper, rushing out of the scullery.

'Be quick about it,' said Mrs Sneed. 'I won't tolerate dilly-dallying, even on a Sunday.' Then she lay back in the chair for another snooze.

Tally hurried into the servants' hall. She passed under the vaulted ceiling and through the carved archway. Her shoes echoed on the stone floor as she moved along the tapestry corridor, filled with statues, ornaments and old wall-hangings. Tally's favourite tapestry was a beautiful embroidery of a garden. Tally loved its stitching, she loved its colours and she loved its images. But most of all, she loved that the tapestry was also a map – a set of clues that she had used to open the trapdoor to

the Secret Library. Now, as she passed by, Tally ran her fingertips along the tasselled wool hem.

Suddenly there were noises from further down the corridor.

Clump. Whump. Wheeze.

'It's Mr Bood,' Tally whispered. 'Oh no! He's bound to give me more chores.'

Squill jumped out of her pinafore pocket and on to a nearby pot plant. He had discovered a very useful weakness in Mr Bood. The butler was terrified of snakes (and spiders and cauliflower). One afternoon, Squill had been dozing in the pantry when Mr Bood came waddling in, hunting for a snack. Mr Bood had taken one look at the long red shape coiled round the bowl of blackberries and screamed, 'Eeek! A snake!'

Ever since that day, whenever Squill saw Mr Bood coming to boss Tally, he would hide and wiggle his tail into view so it looked like the slithering of a snake. It was very effective. So far, he had scared the butler by the willow tree (making him jump into the lake), in the ballroom

(Mr Bood threw himself under the sofa) and in the bath.

(Imagine that scene! Ew! Stop!)

Now, Squill hid behind the plant.

Mr Bood came round the corner.

'Twoolly!' he puffed when he saw Tally. As usual, he had forgotten her name. He wiped his sweaty forehead with his sleeve. Tally winced. She would have to wash that uniform later. 'I need you to ...' Tally groaned inwardly as she waited to hear.

Squill slowly poked his tail out from behind the plant. He wiggled the tip in the air. To Tally, it looked like a furry feather duster, but Mr Bood saw something else.

'Eeek!' he cried. 'A snake!'

He waddled away as quickly as he could (which wasn't very quickly).

'Thanks, Squill!' Tally grinned at the squirrel.

'Tally, help!' came the cry from Lady Beatrice's drawing room.

CHAPTER TWO

Tally found Lady Beatrice perched on the sofa in the blue drawing room. Her back was perfectly straight. She had a silk scarf round her throat and a matching handbag at her feet. She was flicking through the pages of her favourite book, MRS PRIMM'S GUIDE TO BEING A LADY.

It was first published in 1834 and contained many useful pieces of advice, such as:

While at the opera or theatre, ladies must sit on the right of the box, except where there are gentlemen present, in which case a middle seat is more appropriate. If the number of gentlemen in the party is more than the number of ladies, ladies should never sit on the right or the middle but must remain on the left at all times.

As Tally came into the drawing room, Lady Beatrice was nodding to herself while she read (gently, so as not to ruin her hairstyle).

'Oh, there you are.' Lady Beatrice looked up.

'How can I help, my lady?' said Tally.

The mistress of the manor screwed up her face. 'I had a very urgent task for you. It was … It was …' She looked around the room, her shoulders sagging. 'I can't remember what it was …'

'Was it something in your book?' suggested Tally. She pointed at the book, which was open at 0–P.

'Oh yes!' cried Lady Beatrice. She handed the book to Tally. 'Read the top entry to me, will you?'

Tally read out loud. 'P is for pet,' she began.

'All country houses must have a house pet. It makes guests feel welcome and gives the stately mansion a homely feel.'

She read on: 'The house pet should be dressed

in an outfit to match the staff uniforms and may wear a bell, ribbon or collar as appropriate. It should have its own cushion and live near the fire in a public room for added effect.'

'Well?' said Lady Beatrice. 'Now do you see how important this is? I don't have a house pet.' Desperation crept into her voice. 'What kind of pet should I get, Tally?' Lady Beatrice pressed a silk handkerchief to her cheek. 'A horse would take up far too much room, and a chicken just wouldn't suit ribbons.' Lady Beatrice looked around the room and her eyes fixed on Squill, sitting patiently on Tally's shoulder.

'Of course!' cried Lady Beatrice. 'Bring that red thing over here …'

Tally's stomach tightened. 'Sorry, my lady, which red thing?'

'You know, the red wriggly thing on your shoulder.'

'The squirrel?' Tally frowned.

'Yes, yes, whatever. Just pop him on the cushion so I can tie this bit of ribbon round his neck.'

Tally looked at Squill. Squill looked at Tally. Then he quickly lifted up her ponytail and hid behind her hair.

'Now, now, enough silliness,' said Lady Beatrice, reaching out. 'Don't you want to sit on this cushion next to me all day?' she said. 'I've plenty of nuts you can eat. All you have to do in return is mix me a drink every now and then.'

Quick as a flash, Squill leapt up and hung on to the chandelier dangling from the ceiling.

'I don't think he wants to,' said Tally. 'He doesn't really like sitting still.'

'Well, what am I to do, then?' Lady Beatrice's voice began to rise in panic.

Tally thought for a moment. 'What about a dog?' she suggested.

'A dog!' Lady Beatrice's eyes lit up. 'That's a wonderful idea.'

Tally left her telephoning dog breeders.

Bearded Collies – bred by Harris Long
Greyhounds – bred by C. Howie Runs

Guard Dogs – bred by Al Sation
Large Dogs – bred by Ellie Funt

Back in the servants' hall, the sound of the
housekeeper's snores drifted from the kitchen.

'She's asleep!' whispered Tally to Squill.
Maybe she didn't need to get back to the
kitchen so quickly after all. 'Let's go to the
Secret Library! If we hurry, Mrs Sneed will
never even notice. I want to look up more
about dog behaviour for Lord Mollett. And
now she's getting a puppy, Lady Beatrice will
need our help too.'

Squill's black eyes lit up in excitement.

Tally stepped through the courtyard and
into the rose garden. It always smelled so
wonderful here – sweet and musky. Usually
at this time of year, the roses were full of bees
buzzing around collecting nectar, but today
the flowers were strangely quiet. There were
no bees anywhere to be seen. Tally went to the
hives to investigate.

The three white hives sat at the end of the rose garden, between the old malthouse and the infirmary, where monks had once looked after patients. The hives were quiet and still. Puzzled, Tally stepped closer. She peered in. They were completely empty.

'Our bees have gone!' Tally cried. 'Where are they?'

She double-checked every hive. There was no sign of a single bee, but at her feet she spotted a trail in the mud. Tally bent down, rubbing the pale flecks beneath her fingertips. Sawdust. Where had that come from?

'I don't understand. I cleaned the hives yesterday morning and the bees seemed really happy.' Tally frowned. 'There's something funny going on, Squill. Let's look up bees in the Secret Library as well.'

Tally and Squill ran past the malthouse and through the apple orchard. At the end of the estate, where the cliffs met the sea, there stood five enormous stones: four round the outside and one in the centre. These stones hid the entrance to the Secret Library.

Tally's heart always beat that little bit faster the moment she stepped into the stone circle. Here, protected from the sea wind, the air was still and quiet, like the estate was holding its breath. Tally looked up at the ancient grey stones towering over her. They had been here for hundreds of years, keeping the secret of the library safe.

She went straight to the central stone. This one held a puzzle.

Carved into the rough stone were ten holes. Ten little rocks lay in a neat pile next to it, small cubed pieces with images on them. Each cube fitted into one of the holes in the stone – but it had taken Tally ages to work out which cube went into which hole.

Tally hummed a song under her breath. Ma had taught it to her eight years ago, when Tally was just a little girl. It helped her remember how to order the cubes.

Give me your hand and we'll run
Down past the grass, up through the trees.

Tally picked out the cube engraved with the outline of a hand, and placed it into the first middle hole. Then she put the grass one under it, and the tree one above it.

Give me your time and we'll sail
Down to the boat, up on the seas.

One by one, Tally inserted the cubes.

Give me your heart and we'll fly
Up like a bee, down under leaves
This is the answer I know
This is the truth I will see
This is the way I will go
Down where the gate waits for me.

Tally fitted the last one, the one that
looked like a gate, into the
bottom-right hole.

There was a shudder and a
creak as a hidden trapdoor by
the stone slid back to reveal a
dark hole in the ground.

The entrance to the Secret
Library was open!

CHAPTER THREE

Tally lowered herself into the darkness, her toes searching for the first rung of the rope ladder. For a second, her feet swung in mid-air, then … phew … the tip of her toe touched the wood.

Rung by rung, she felt her way down, Squill hanging on with his paws around her neck.

At the bottom, Tally stepped on to the stone floor. It smelled musty down here, the air filled with the dusty scent of ancient paper.

Tally walked past the library rules:

There will be only one Secret Keeper in each generation.

The Secret Keeper must be under the age of thirteen.

The Keeper must guard the secret of the library and the information within.

Talking is permitted.

She lit the lamps one by one and the old library was flooded with soft light.

Crazy shelves twisted this way and that, in aisle after aisle. The hidden books were filled with spidery writing, and covered in leather or paper or wood. Some were held together with string, and some with ribbon. There were even a few old wax tablets in wooden cases that looked really ancient.

Tally moved along the
shelves, stopping at:

ANIMALS (Aardvark to Zebra)

She ran her finger along the
spines, passing the 'A's …

AARDVARK
ABYSSINIAN GRASS RAT
ADDER
AFRICAN ELEPHANT
ARCTIC HARE
ASIATIC BLACK BEAR
AZUMI SHREW

… to the 'B's, until she found:

BEES by A. Piary

Tally sat down on the dusty floor. Her heart
was beating faster. The Secret Library was a
special place, a place where books became more
than just words on a page.

'Ready?' she asked Squill. He was chewing the
tip of his tail with excitement.

Tally heaved open the large book and read the first words out loud.

'*Honeybees are insects.*'

The library lamps flickered and Tally felt a thrill run through her. The magic was beginning!

All at once a hologram[2] of a bee floated up out of the book.

The bee looked so real. Up close, she could see the insect was divided into three parts: a head, a furry bit of body and a hard part, covered in black stripes. Even though she knew it was just a moving image, Tally gasped to see it so close. The bee's wings were quivering, making its little furry body vibrate just by her nose.

'*Bees have six legs, two pairs of wings and ... oh ... FIVE eyes!*' she read out, and the bee turned its body slowly round in the air so Tally could count.

[2] A hologram is a three-dimensional (3D) image.

'They are social insects, which means they live with thousands of other honeybees in a group called a colony. The honeybees work together to build honeycomb nests and make honey.'

A giant tree rose up from the page. Attached to one of its branches was a hive – it looked like a slice of honeycomb covered in a mass of bees. The sound of buzzing grew louder as more bee holograms filled the air, busy doing jobs. The worker bees were female, Tally learned. These bees are the ones that gather pollen and nectar from the flowers.

'Ooh, Squill! It says here that when a bee finds honey, she does a little dance to tell the other bees.'[3]

Now, the hologram changed to a field of brightly coloured flowers. A warm breeze floated through the air, fluffing up the ends of Tally's curls. One of the bees landed on a flower and waggled her body, then moved in a circle and waggled again. The other bees flew over to join her.

'Each colony smells different so the bees can find their way home,' she read as she watched the bees

[3] This dance is called a 'waggle'. The bee dances in a figure of eight.

gathering the pollen and nectar before flying back to their hive.

'*It is rare for honeybees to leave their hive. They are very attached to their home and only move away if there are problems, such as no food, bad weather or disease. Some scientists think bees can even recognise the faces of the humans who look after them.*'[4]

Tally closed the book and at once the hologram bees disappeared.

'I don't understand why our bees left, Squill,' said Tally sadly. 'I thought I looked after them well. We have lovely roses and sweet apples in the orchard. Their hive was clean and safe.' She gave a little sniff. 'I really did love them.'[4]

Squill snuggled closer to her.

'We just have to hope they come back,' Tally said. 'Come on. Let's find out more about dogs now to cheer ourselves up. We can help Lord Mollett with his book and Lady Beatrice with her puppy.'

[4] A scientist put photographs of faces up on a board and gave the bees sugar when they flew to one particular face. Soon he found the bees flew to that face nearly all of the time.

Tally read along the spines until she reached:
DOGS by Fred Setter

'Here we are!'

Squill settled down with his chin on his paw
to listen.

'*Dogs have a very loyal character,*' she read
out. '*They protect the humans they live with and
give friendship and love.*'

A hologram shimmered in the air before
them. It was a large yellow dog. He had bright
brown eyes and soft white fur on his tummy. He
wagged his tail and sank down next to Tally, his
velvet ears flopping on to the dusty floor.

'*Some dogs are extremely intelligent. They can
be trained to help blind people
find their way. They know
how to lead their human
up and down steps
and in between
obstacles.*'

As Tally read this bit aloud, the dog next to her jumped up. By his side stood a young boy, holding a lead with a special flat handle. Instantly a hologram of a forest appeared in the Secret Library, tall trees filling the aisles. Tally could smell fresh pine leaves. The dog cleverly led the boy through the forest, avoiding fallen logs and low branches.

'Wow!' Tally whispered.

She turned the page and the forest disappeared.

'Thank you!' Tally called as the dog hologram faded away.

Tally hugged her knees tightly to her chest. Reading made Tally feel close to her mother. Ma had been a Secret Keeper too. She had known about the Secret Library. On the day she disappeared, eight years ago, she'd brought Tally to the cliff to show her the ancient stones.

Ma had often made up stories for Tally. They were about a bear who liked wearing different outfits. Ma had sewn Tally her own little cloth teddy bear. 'I'm going on an adventure!' Mr Bear would say, putting on a sailor hat or a beret and heading out the door. That bear had been one of Tally's most treasured possessions. Until Mrs Sneed had thrown it over the cliff.

Tally gave a little shudder and rubbed the bit of old lace in her pocket, lace from the hem of Ma's skirt. It was all she had left of her mother now.

There was a muffled *ding dong*. The church bell was ringing in the nearby village. Tally froze and counted the chimes.

'Six o'clock! Oh no. Squill, we have to get back and peel the potatoes for dinner!'

CHAPTER FOUR

The next day, Tally couldn't settle to her
chores. She went from room to room, wiping
a mantelpiece here, dusting a cushion there,
but she couldn't concentrate enough to clean
properly. All she could think about was the bees.
She gave up on the inside of the house and took
her mop and bucket into the garden.

The roses looked so lonely. Their bee friends
still hadn't come back.

'Let's do some work out here, Squill,' she said.
'That way, we'll spot the bees if they do return.'

All morning while Tally cleaned the fountain,
Squill ran back and forth to the hives, his little body
curving like a wave as he bounded over the grass.

'Anything?' asked Tally for the tenth time. The squirrel shook his head.

Tally sighed and wiped the Cupid statue inside the fountain pool. She was just cleaning his left leg when the bell rang at the manor-house gate.

'Tally!' came a shout from the kitchen window. Mrs Sneed's sleepy head popped out. 'Go and answer the door, you lazy girl. Whoever rang the bell just woke me up.'

Tally dashed into the servants' hall and took the gate key from the hook.

She set off down the drive, Squill riding on her shoulder. As they drew closer to the manor gate, Tally could see someone standing behind the iron bars.

'It's the postman!' she cried. In his hands he held a basket with a ribbon round the handle.

'Package for her ladyship,' he said.

Squeeeaaaak went the rusty old gate as Tally opened it.

'Thank you!' she said. She took the basket and locked the gate again.

A noise came
from the basket
and Tally lifted the lid.
Inside she found a white
ball of fluff that yapped and barked.

'It's Lady Beatrice's puppy!'

Squill stared down from Tally's shoulder, a
suspicious look on his face.

'What do you think of him, Squill?' asked Tally.

Squill jumped on to the handle of the basket to
get a closer look. The puppy reached his head out
and gave the squirrel an enormous lick, covering
him in slobber from head to tail. Tally burst out
laughing as Squill wiped himself clean with the
corner of her pinafore.

'He likes you!' she said.

The squirrel chattered crossly and hid in Tally's
pocket.

'Yip!' the puppy barked.

'Hello!' laughed Tally as the puppy jumped out
of the basket and jiggled in her arms, licking her
face. 'I'd better take you to Lady Beatrice.'

She put the puppy down, and he ran round and round until he tripped over his ears.

Tally giggled and the puppy wagged his tail at top speed, thumping the ground. He stopped for a moment, confused by where the thumping sound was coming from, then thumped his tail again. Stop. Thump. Stop. Thump. He would have gone on like that all day if Tally hadn't picked him up and put him back in the basket.

Tally carried him through the manor house.

'Yip!'

The puppy was so excited to see his new home.

'Yap!'

He barked at everything.

Tally knocked on Lady Beatrice's door.

'Your ladyship?' she called. 'The puppy is here.'

She opened the door gently. Lady Beatrice was still in bed, with a breakfast tray on her lap. She was wearing a silk nightgown, a lacy dressing gown and a smart hat. The hat had a stiff, wide brim, covered in layers of flowers and ribbons.

As she nibbled her toast, the flowers bobbed
their heads up and down.

The second he spied the toast, the puppy gave a
bark and leapt from the basket onto the bed.

'Aaaaghhhh!' screamed Lady Beatrice.

'Yap!' the puppy barked through a mouthful of
crumbs.

'What is this?' Lady Beatrice watched in horror
as the white fluffy thing slurped her tea.

'It's the house pet,' said Tally. 'Remember? You
ordered a dog yesterday.'

'Oh yes,' said Lady Beatrice, after a pause. She
cocked her head on one side. 'It isn't very big.'

'He will grow,' said Tally.

'Really?' Lady Beatrice
didn't look so sure.

'Yes, your
ladyship. I am
certain of it.'

The puppy began to scamper on the bed, pouncing on mounds of duvet and rolling on his back. 'Gruff!'

'I think you'd better take him away now,' said Lady Beatrice faintly. 'And I'm going to need a new cup of tea.'

'Yes, your ladyship,' said Tally. She scooped up the puppy and he nuzzled into her arms.

Tally's mind flitted back to her own first time at Mollett Manor. She'd toddled after Mrs Sneed that day, sniffing and still looking back for Ma. Through the woods they'd walked, past the malthouse, past the beehives, past the rose bushes. From there, she'd had her first glimpse of the manor house. The old monastery was soft and yellow, the grand entrance welcoming her in. Little Tally had heard the bees buzzing hello. As she'd stepped on to the ancient stone cobbles in the courtyard, a warm feeling had filled Tally's tummy. That was the moment she knew the manor was special.

'Woof!' said the puppy now as he licked her neck.

Tally smiled at him – she was going to make sure he felt welcome at Mollett Manor. As she headed through the door, Tally paused and looked back. 'Lady Beatrice? What would you like to call your new dog?'

Lady Beatrice gazed at the little bundle of fur. 'He shall be Lord William Horatio Mollett – after my grandfather.'

'O … K.' Tally nodded slowly. 'Shall we call him William for short?'

'Yes,' answered Lady Beatrice, the flowers on her hat bobbing again, 'except on special occasions.'

The first few days were messy. William weed everywhere. He weed a little puddle on the kitchen floor and on Lady Beatrice's antique sofa. He left an even yuckier present in Mr Bood's shoes.

'Eh? What's this? Tully! Come and clean this up at once!'

In the end, Tally and Squill nicknamed William 'Widdles'.

'It's not really his fault,' she explained to Squill, as she cuddled the little puppy. 'He's only a baby. He'll learn.'

Squill gave a shrug as if to say, *I hope so.*

Tally did all of the work looking after and training Widdles. She was exhausted! Widdles was very cute, but he was also the silliest dog you could ever meet. Once, he had hiccups and spent all morning barking at whoever was making that funny noise.

'Hic! Yap! Hic! Yip!'

Squill buried his head in his paws.

Now that she remembered ordering him, Lady Beatrice adored Widdles.

'Mummy's iddle baby!' she said every morning, smothering his pink nose with kisses. 'Cutie, cutie pie.' Of course, she didn't have to clean up the puddles.

One evening, Tally brought Widdles's meal to the dining room, served on his own crystal plate.

Lady Beatrice had drawn up an elaborate menu:

Monday –	*Seared sirloin steak enveloped in slow-poached beef jus*
Tuesday –	*Hand-carved gourmet bone drizzled with turkey emulsion*
Wednesday –	*Smoked rabbit resting on a bed of pigeon foam*
Thursday –	*Chicken fricassée au lord garnished with a sprinkling of crispy bacon*
Friday –	*Deconstructed pork pie enrobed in chicken pâté*

Today was Thursday, so Widdles was having chicken. He had his own place at the table, right next to Lady Beatrice, and he was waiting patiently with a napkin tied round his neck. Well, kind of patiently. Tally groaned as she saw him nibbling the tablecloth.

Tally was supposed to stand at the door of the dining room with the plate. She had to give Lord Mollett a signal with her eyebrows so he could then ring a little bell on the table next to him.

The lord was testing the new theory from Ivan Pavlov that dogs can learn to anticipate their dinner. He had a notebook ready to write down his observations.

Now, as soon as he heard the bell, Widdles began to bark in excitement. Tally put his dinner in front of him and he gobbled it all down in five seconds flat.

'Well done, William,' Lord Mollett said as he made a note. 'Look, Tally, that's three times in a row he's known his dinner was coming.' He scribbled something else down. 'But he doesn't get many marks for table manners,' he said sadly as Widdles began to lick the salt and pepper pots.

'Oh, he's perfect the way he is!' cried Lady Beatrice. Her face shone.

Lord Mollett smiled. 'It's lovely to see you so content, Beatrice,' he said.

'I love Lord William so much,' Lady Beatrice declared. 'He's the best thing that ever happened to me! In fact, I've decided to give him one of the family pendants. Tally, could you get mine, please?'

'Yes, your ladyship,' said Tally. The Mollett brother and sister each had a pendant. They were family heirlooms, passed down through generations of Molletts. Each pendant was round and gold, like a coin. On one side was printed: '**MOLLETT MANOR**'. On the other was the family motto, **SEMPER MUTA TOGULAM** which, Tally knew from her lessons with Lord Mollett, was Latin for 'Always change your underpants.'

The pendants lived with the other precious things in the cabinet outside Lord Mollett's study. Tally knew them well because she polished them every week. She reached inside the cabinet and took Lady Beatrice's. It felt smooth and warm in her hand as her fingers closed around the gold.

'Here it is,' she said, coming back into the dining room.

Lady Beatrice tried to hang the pendant on Widdles's collar, which was not an easy task as the puppy kept licking her hand.

'That tickles!' cried Lady Beatrice,

collapsing in giggles. But eventually, the pendant was in place and William looked very smart indeed. *You'd almost never know he was such a silly dog,* Tally thought.

'He's very spoilt,' Lord Mollett laughed, peering over the top of his glasses. His eyes were twinkling and Tally could tell he didn't really mind.

'No, he isn't!' Lady Beatrice protested, pulling the puppy to her so that he almost disappeared into her bosom. 'He's the house pet and he needs to look his best for visitors.'

Tally looked out of the window at the manor's gravelled drive. She couldn't remember the last time they'd had visitors, but knew not to say anything. Lord Mollett and Lady Beatrice were happy, and that was all that mattered.

CHAPTER FIVE

On Friday afternoon, Tally took Widdles for
a walk in the village. She walked him out of the
servants' hall, through the courtyard and up
to the high wall of the manor house. Then she
unlocked the big, heavy gate. It squeaked loudly
as it opened on its rusty hinges.

Widdles was very excited as they set off. He
pulled and yanked on the lead, desperate to
sniff every smell, bite every stick and roll in
every puddle.

They walked on through the village,
    down the lane,
        past an old church and
            alongside the playground.

They stopped for a rest outside a school. Tally leaned against the railings. For a moment, she wondered about how her life might have been different had Ma still been around. They might be living in a little cottage in a village just like this one. Ma would do sewing or teaching, and Tally would go to school, with a white cotton apron, a slate and an inkwell all of her own. But … then she'd never have found the Secret Library.

'I bet none of those schoolchildren has ever seen a tiger, Squill,' she whispered. Squill gave a shiver, remembering the day a huge, snarling beast had floated out of one of the library books, twitching its stripy tail.

'Hello,' came a shy voice. A little boy was walking down the lane towards her, holding a poster. 'I'm Adam. Have you seen my guinea pig? He went missing last Saturday.' He showed Tally the poster as he pinned it to the lamppost.

MISSING: ONE BROWN GUINEA PIG WITH A WHITE TUMMY. ANSWERS TO THE NAME OF MR NIBBLES.

'Oh, poor Mr Nibbles,' said Tally. 'I'm sorry, I haven't seen him.'

Adam's eyes filled with tears.

'I'll look out for him, I promise,' said Tally.

'Will you?' Adam looked at her. 'If you find him, bring him back to my cottage there – the one with the blue door.' The boy pointed. Tally nodded. Now she had three animals to find: Mrs Marsh's cat, Adam's guinea pig and the manor-house bees.

Tally led Widdles through the village into the park. As they walked, they came across a small wooden train. The train was made of low carriages – each one came to the height of Tally's knee. At the front of the train was a large wagon. Across it was painted:

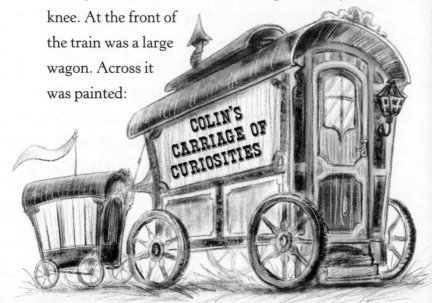

COLIN'S
CARRIAGE OF
CURIOSITIES

A horse grazed nearby.

'Oh. This must be the travelling show!' Tally cried. She stopped to look in all the carriages.

Each one held a wooden cage lined with sawdust. Inside every cage was an animal.

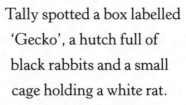

Tally spotted a box labelled 'Gecko', a hutch full of black rabbits and a small cage holding a white rat.

'Brie,' Tally read from the sign under the rat's cage.

The little creature looked up at the sound of her name. She had a twitchy pink nose and ruby-coloured eyes. Tally glanced from animal to animal.

'None of them seems happy.' Tally bit her lip. 'I'm glad I didn't go to the show after all.'

Squill stroked the little rat through the bars, and Widdles gave it a lick, then ran behind a tree to bark at a shadow.

Tally looked up to see a man walking towards her, kicking sawdust off his boots. He was tall and skinny with a narrow face and hair greased down flat against his skull. He yanked the horse's head up from the grass and led him towards the carriage. This must be Colin, she thought.

'What do you want?' he growled, drawing closer to Tally.

'I was just looking at your lovely rabbits,' she replied quickly.

'Lazy rabbits, more like. Practise those backflips again,' he snarled, banging the hutch with his fist and sending the frightened rabbits scattering. 'We've been here a week since the last show doing our training. We leave for the next village on Sunday and the animals aren't even ready to perform.'

Squill gave a disapproving squeak from behind Tally's ponytail. Colin's beady eyes lit up.

'That's a fine specimen you have there,' he said. His voice softened and he leaned towards the squirrel. 'Red squirrels are very rare, you know.'

'He's not a "specimen",' Tally said. 'He's my friend.'

Squill dived from Tally's shoulder to land behind her legs.

'Clever, too.' Colin stroked his stubbly chin.

Tally drew back. There was something funny about Colin. He was full of bottled-up energy, like a jack-in-the-box ready to spring.

A squeak came from the white rat in the cage.

'Quiet, you!' shouted Colin. 'You're only supposed to be using your voice for singing.'

The rat sniffed.

A long meow came from the next carriage along.

'And you, pesky cat! Get back to work!'

'Don't shout at the animals,' said Tally bravely. 'They don't like it.'

'Pah!' Colin waved his hand.

The horse gave a sad whinny.

'Shush,' snapped Colin. 'You've had enough grass. We're off round the village again in a minute.'

'We have to go now. Goodbye,' said Tally,

turning to leave.

Widdles came bounding back from behind the tree.

'What a pretty dog!' Colin bent down and peered at the pendant round Widdles's neck. 'Mollett Manor,' he read slowly. 'Yes, I know that estate.'

'We need to go now,' Tally said again to her friends. She felt a weight in her pocket as Squill jumped in. He seemed slightly heavier than usual, but Tally didn't stop to check why.

She ran across the park, pulling Widdles down the lane and into the grounds of Mollett Manor as quickly as she could. Then she locked the gate shut behind her.

Tally hung the gate key back on its hook and sat on the kitchen floor, shaking with anger. Those poor animals! That Colin was such a horrid man. There was a high squeak from her pinafore pocket. Tally frowned. That didn't sound like Squill. She opened the big, wide pocket at the front to see a flash of red fur … and something white.

'Come out,' said Tally gently.
'We won't hurt you.'

Slowly a furry body emerged.
It was Brie, the rat. She had
a sweet little face, and her
eyes pleaded with Tally.

'Did you help her
escape?' Tally asked
Squill. He gave a sheepish shrug.

All at once there was the sharp sound of shoes
tapping on the stones.

'Mrs Sneed!' cried Tally. If the housekeeper
found a rat in here, she wouldn't be happy. Tally
glanced nervously at the large knife left out on
the chopping block.

'We've got to take you somewhere safe,' said
Tally. She grabbed an empty box.

'Quick!' she cried. Brie scrambled in, quivering
with fear.

The footsteps were getting closer and closer.

'Let's take her to the stables,' Tally told Squill.
'We'll go through the secret passage so no one

sees us.' Squill leapt on to her shoulder. Widdles just looked confused.

As quickly as she could, Tally hurried to the archway at the back of the scullery. Above the fireplace, letters carved in the stone spelled out 'Experts snoop.' It was a puzzle, one that only Tally had solved. Rearranged, the letters spelled 'Press X to open.' With trembling fingers, Tally pressed the 'X' and the stone slid open.

Tally balanced the box on her hip and stepped into the dark passage.

'Hurry! Hurry!' She pulled Widdles in after her and silently begged the secret door to close. Just in time, the door slid shut. In the darkness, from the passage behind the fireplace, Tally could hear Mrs Sneed calling for her in the kitchen.

'Phew. That was close,' she whispered. She turned her lamp up high. There was a little wriggle from the box on her hip.

'Don't be afraid,' Tally told Brie. 'I know this tunnel well.'

On went the tunnel, deep under the grounds

of the ancient manor house. Tally's footsteps echoed on the old cobblestones, Squill brushed the cobwebs with his tail, and Widdles tripped over his ears.

Before long, the passage began to slope uphill and Tally gave the stone door at the end a hard push. They came out in the fireplace of the old infirmary. Tally closed the door behind her and it locked fast.

'It's not far to the stables from here, Brie,' she said, moving along the rows of old iron bedframes.

Tally pushed open the infirmary door into the garden and headed past the malthouse and alongside the apple orchard. Brie poked her twitchy nose out of the box, sniffing at the air.

'Yes, there are lots of lovely apples for you to eat,' Tally told her. 'Take the ones on the ground, but leave the soft ones for the bees.' Her voice faltered. 'In … in case they ever come back.'

Tally nudged the stable door open with her foot and set the box down. The stable smelled warm

and musty. These days, it was just used as a
storeroom, and no one came in here except Tally.

'Welcome to your new home!'

Brie crept out nervously and looked around.
She saw the piles of straw where she could hide,
and the logs where she could jump about
and play. She watched Tally
tying a little hammock for
her, made out of an old scarf.
Then she jumped up and
down squeaking her thanks.

'You're welcome,' said
Tally, bending down to pat her.

Brie rubbed her face against Tally's shoe.

'I'll check on you later,' said Tally as she closed
the stable door. 'You'll be safe here. Just don't
go exploring.' She set off back to the manor,
humming a little tune.

Later that night, Tally set Widdles down to
sleep on his velvet cushion, pulling the cashmere
blanket up around his ears.

'Sleep tight!' she whispered.

In her little sink bed, Tally settled down
between the taps. She could hear Squill snoring
softly next to her and Widdles giving little puppy
whimpers as he dreamed of chasing rabbits.

Tally smiled. She might not have a mother or a
father, but she had a little family all of her own.

CHAPTER SIX

'Tally?' said Lord Mollett.

Tally looked up from Lord Mollett's desk. She was supposed to be listening to his lesson on the French Revolution, but her mind was busy thinking about other things: things like the Carriage of Curiosities, and Brie, and the missing bees.

'Sorry – I, er … What were you saying?' Tally's cheeks blushed with guilt. She usually loved these lessons!

'Let's leave the revolution for now,' Lord Mollett said kindly. He opened a handkerchief full of blackberries and Squill squeaked in delight.

Tally smiled gratefully. Lord Mollett was always so kind to Squill. She thought about

Widdles, downstairs in the kitchen. Lord Mollett had asked Mrs Sneed to look after him. The housekeeper had scowled, her spiky face screwed up tight as she'd tried to think of a way of getting out of it. But she'd been forced to take the wriggling Widdles from Lord Mollett. Hopefully the puppy was behaving himself now – and not jumping on to the counter to swipe a piece of bacon.

'What do you think I should put in this chapter about using cutlery?' Lord Mollett shuffled through the notes for his book.

'Has William shown any signs of getting to grips with a knife and fork?'

'Well,' said Tally, remembering how the puppy had run off with a fork and buried it in the mud the other day, 'he ... um ... seems enthusiastic ...'

'Edward! Edward!' called a voice from the corridor. 'I've had a fabulous idea!' Lady Beatrice burst through the study door. 'Let's have a tea party! Then everyone can meet Lord William!'

Lord Mollett opened his mouth in surprise. Tally stared at Lady Beatrice. Visitors? At Mollett Manor?

'We used to have parties all the time!' Lady Beatrice cried. 'Do you remember?'

'I do,' said her brother warmly. 'I think that's a super idea.'

'Oh, Tally.' Lady Beatrice turned to her. 'Can we have it tomorrow? Can you get started right away? Please?' Lady Beatrice looked so happy. Her face was glowing.

'Of course I will,' Tally answered.

Lady Beatrice clapped her hands. 'I'll telephone everyone we know!'

When Tally walked back into the kitchen, Mrs Sneed was asleep in the armchair.

'Where's William?' she asked.

The housekeeper started awake. 'Oh,' she said, looking around. 'He's just gone for a little walk.

I'm sure he'll come back.'

Tally and Squill looked for Widdles as they carried out the tables for the party.

They looked for him as they tied ribbons to the trees.

They looked for him as they followed Mrs Sneed's long list of chores.

By dinnertime, Tally and Squill were exhausted.

And they hadn't seen Widdles for hours.

'Where is he, Squill? He's usually around our feet wanting tummy tickles or snacks to eat.'

Tally nibbled the side of her thumb. 'Let's ask Lady Beatrice if she's seen him.'

'I'm so excited about the party tomorrow,' Lady Beatrice cried when Tally walked into the blue drawing room. 'Aren't you? Everyone's coming! I can't wait to show them all how cute

Lord William is!'

'Um … yes …' said Tally. 'Er … have you
seen Widdles … I mean William … recently?'

'No,' said Lady Beatrice, her smile fading.
'Where is he?'

'I … I don't know,' answered Tally.

Lady Beatrice went pale. All the happiness
went out of her like water draining down a sink.
'Does that mean he's lost? Oh, he's lost. Oh,
Lord William. Oh nooooo!' Lady Beatrice lay
back on the sofa with her hands over her face.
'What shall I do?'

Lord Mollett rushed into the drawing room.
Lady Beatrice sobbed.

'Oh, my poor puppy! Where is he?'

'Now, Beatrice,' said Lord Mollett, 'don't
make yourself ill. We'll find him. Tally will find
him. Won't you, Tally?'

Tally and Squill ran through every corner of
Mollett Manor, from the stables to the herb
gardens.

'Widdles! Widdles! Widdles!' Tally called.

There was no sign of him, and now the sun was going down.

Tally's eyes filled with tears. Squill chirruped. He jumped on to her shoulder and reached his little paw up to stroke her head.

'I hope he hasn't wiggled out of the manor and got himself lost in the village.'

Squill raised his eyebrows as if to say, *Well, that's perfectly possible.*

'We need some kind of high place so we can see across the whole village at once. Oh!' Tally remembered something. Past the infirmary, by the eastern edge of the sea cliffs, was a tall tower. It was once used by the monks as a lighthouse. 'We'd see much better from up there,' she said, gathering her skirts. Squill dived into her pinafore pocket and together they ran to the tower.

Tally walked the whole way round its circular base. In one side there was a door that was locked fast. Round the frame were cobwebs and dust. No one had been up there in years. Tally had never even seen a key.

'Hmmm,' she said. 'I wonder if there's a code to get into this building.' Tally thought through the other codes she had cracked. There was:

The anagram code that opened the tunnel from the scullery to the infirmary.

The magic square that unlocked the passage between the red bedroom and the drawing room.

Then, of course, there was the cubed puzzle for the Secret Library.

Was the tower door another mystery to solve?

She wiped her hand over the door, clearing the dust. There were shapes carved into the stone frame: a square, a rectangle, a trapezoid, a rhombus, a pentagon, a parallelogram, a quadrilateral, a kite, a—

'Wait!' Tally stopped. She looked at the shapes again. With one finger she gently stroked the pentagon. 'There's something funny about this one, Squill,' she said.

Squill leapt on to her shoulder. He leaned closer to the stone shapes and cocked his head to one side.

'Every other shape has four sides. All except this one.' She ran her fingers round the edges of the shape. 'A pentagon has five sides, Squill.'

Squill tried to look wise.

'This shape doesn't belong with the others.' Tally tried to move it sideways. She tapped it. She tried to pull it out. Then ... she pushed it. With a low squeak, the stone shape pressed into the doorframe.

There was a shudder and a whirr. Then a soft click.

The door to the tower swung open inwards.

Tally looked at Squill. Squill looked at Tally.

'We've cracked another code!' she cried.

They stepped into the old tower. It smelled

musty and strange. Tally left the door open so they could see their way. They shuffled across the dusty stone floor to a set of steep spiral stairs. Tally looked up to see a square of light high above her.

Finally they reached the top. The tower was open up here, surrounded by a low wall cut in a crenellation pattern.[5] The sea wind blew fiercely, tangling Tally's curls. She tucked her hair behind her ears and walked closer to the wall. Her breath caught in her throat. They were so high up she felt lightheaded – she could see for miles! How would she find the puppy in all that land?

Squill gave a squeak. Tally looked down. He was jumping up and down on a wooden box.

'What's in there?' Tally crouched down and opened the lid. Inside, nestled in red velvet, was a spyglass. She lifted it out. The brass twinkled in the last of the sunlight. Tally lifted it to her eye and scanned the manor grounds. The spyglass showed her the roses, the beehives, the fountain – but no puppy.

[5]A crenellation pattern leaves regular spaces for arrows to be fired.

Tally turned towards the village. The setting sun glowed on the roofs of the houses, turning them a soft orange. She ran the spyglass over the lane, past the schoolhouse to the park, but there was no sign of Widdles.

Slowly she turned in a circle. As she passed over the cliff, she stopped.

'That's strange.'

She could see something at the cliff edge. It was a long, thin shape, hanging over the cliff, swaying back and forth in the wind.

'Let's go and investigate!'

CHAPTER SEVEN

Tally and Squill ran from the tower towards the stone circle. Soon they reached the bit of land where Tally had spotted the shape.

The edge of the cliff was cordoned off, with a sign that read, 'Danger! No entry.'

This was where Ma had fallen. In her hazy memory, Tally saw Ma leaning over the cliff, searching with her hands. Then she'd stumbled … and Tally had never seen her again.

Tally shook her head to clear it. Usually she avoided coming to the cliff edge. It brought back too many memories. She only came here when she absolutely had to, like last Saturday morning, when Mr Bood had made her trim the lawn all the way to the cliff with scissors.

Tally frowned. Just past the cordon, something metal was shining. Something that definitely hadn't been there on Saturday morning.

Carefully Tally lifted the cordon and crept closer to the edge. Stuck fast into the ground were two iron hooks. Rope was twined round each one.

'These are grappling hooks,' Tally told Squill. 'They're holding a rope ladder – that's what we saw from the top of the tower!'

Tally peered over the cliff. The ladder swung in the breeze. She tried to imagine climbing down it towards the ocean, but the thought made her dizzy. She pulled away, and as the setting sun broke through the clouds, a glint of gold caught her eye. Nestling beside one of the grappling hooks was a round gold pendant. A pendant that read **SEMPER MUTA TOGULAM.**

Tally bent down, scanning the earth for other clues. There was a sprinkling of sawdust by a tree. Sawdust.

There had been sawdust by the bees. And sawdust in the Carriage of Curiosities.

A cold feeling spread over her.

Colin.

All at once images of missing animals filled her mind.

Mrs Marsh's cat.

Adam's guinea pig.

The manor bees.

'Squill,' she said in a small voice, 'I think Widdles has been dognapped!'

Squill squeaked in outrage.

Tally looked down. The tide was out and in the last lights of sunset Tally could see the rocks below. Did Colin use that ladder to get to the manor grounds? Tally squinted. It looked like the ladder went straight down to the rocks and the sea. But that couldn't be right. Thieves didn't just disappear into the ocean – not with a puppy!

She picked up Squill and burrowed her face into his red fur as she thought hard.

'We have to find out more,' she whispered. 'We need the Secret Library!'

In the library, Tally and Squill sat cuddled in an old blanket surrounded by books.

'We have to find something to help us trace the route Colin took. We think he used the rope ladder. But where did he go when he got to the bottom?'

She spread the books out in front of her.

She had:

Books on ants and how they follow trails made by their colony.[6]

Books on swallows and how they know which way to fly.[7]

Books on salmon and how they find their way home.[8]

'What we need is some kind of tracking ability …' Tally remembered reading about scenting, about how dogs can follow smells to find someone. 'Here!' She pounced on a book she'd seen before:

[6] Ants leave a chemical trail to show others where food can be found.
[7] Birds use the position of the sun or the stars to help them find their way.
[8] Salmon return to where they were born to lay their eggs.

TRACKING ANIMALS by Ivor Cent

The book was all about the bloodhound, a large dog that was an expert tracker.

'This is the book for us, Squill!'

Tally pulled the blanket around them both. It was chilly down here at night! The cover of the old book gave a creak as it opened. Tally began to read.

'Human noses work by smelling a chemical in the air. Scent receptors in your nose send signals to your brain, building up a pattern of a smell.'

A huge nose floated up out of the book. Tally could see all the way inside, to the tiny hairs poking out of the pink skin.[9]

She wrinkled her forehead in concentration.

'Humans have around five million scent receptors,' she read. *'They are located high up in the nose.'*

---

[9] These hairs catch bits of dust to stop them entering the lungs.

The image of the nose grew bigger, showing Tally all the way to the back.

'Ew,' she said. 'It's a bit icky up there! *Dogs have around 220 million scent receptors. That's more than forty times the number we have.*'

She turned a page.

'*The bloodhound is the dog with the most sensitive nose.*'

An enormous dog floated up from the book. He had big, droopy cheeks and eyes that nearly disappeared into the folds of his face. Tally had to step back to see him properly.

'It says here that bloodhounds can sniff a person's scent in the air. Our smell is made of sweat, skin and breath. Ew.'

Squill shook his head as if to say; *Humans. Aren't they disgusting?*

The bloodhound put his nose to the ground. His long, floppy ears draped across the floor either side of his nose.

'Those ears help fan the scent towards him,' whispered Tally.

'Bloodhounds have very loose, flappy skin, which curves around their nose and traps the scent.'

The dog gave a loud sniff. Tally could hear the air moving across his nostrils.

'A bloodhound's brain takes a "smell photo" of the person and he can follow the trail in the air for miles.'

The huge dog sniffed the air, then bounded off, racing up and down the library, his nose to the ground and his massive feet thudding as he ran.

She closed the book and the dog disappeared.

'That's what we need to find Widdles,' said Tally. 'A bloodhound nose. Surely there's something to help us somewhere in this magical place ...'

Tally searched the shelves. Squill clambered up higher and higher, following the twisting conga line of books. He squeaked down at Tally and she pushed the library ladder over towards him.

'What have you found?' she said, climbing up the ladder to join him.

Up here the books were dustier. Specks of fluff glistened in the lamplight as they floated past Tally's nose.

Squill was pointing his paw at a dark purple book that was thinner than the rest. The book glowed, shining against the other spines. She drew it out.

THE SECRETS OF SCENTING by Kay Nine

The friends looked at each other. With Squill perched on her shoulder, Tally climbed down the ladder. She opened the cover of the book and read the introduction.

'*Scientists have tried to copy the bloodhound nose in order to detect things like bombs and even diseases.*[10] Imagine that, Squill! A dog could sniff out whether you were about to come down with measles!' Squill nodded wisely, even though he had no idea what measles were.

[10] This is true. Scent hounds are used to search for injured people in earthquakes, to track down escaped prisoners and to check for weapons at airports. Scientists are trying to make a machine that can do this job just as well so they can send it into caves or danger zones.

Some kind of nut maybe?[11]

'*This book will tell you how to make a nose for tracking. But you must promise never to give the secret away.*'

Tally knew what to do. Without her promise, the pages of the book would be stuck fast together.

'I promise,' she whispered solemnly.

The book gave a soft sigh, and the next page flicked open by itself.

Tally grinned at Squill. She took a breath and began to read.

'*How to make a super-nose.*'

A little shiver ran down her spine.

She needed to make a special kind of funnel. It had to have big flaps like the bloodhound nose to hold the scent in, and it had to be able to suck in more smell than a human nose. *What could I use to make it?*

'We could build a cone out of stiff paper,' she said. 'I could sew long scarves round the base to make the loose, wrinkly skin. And Lord Mollett

---

[11] No, Squill. They are not.

has a skiing hat with ear flaps. That might do!'

But the most important thing Tally needed was sniffing sense – a special, magical substance to make the nose work. Without this, it would be just a paper funnel.

'*Sniffing sense must be granted willingly by an animal with a good sense of smell,*' Tally read. 'Oh, Squill,' she said in dismay. 'How are we going to get the sniffing sense? We don't have a bloodhound at Mollett Manor.'

The book turned its own page, and Tally learned something important:

Dogs aren't the only animals good at scenting.

'There's a list of top sniffers here,' said Tally. 'It says that squirrels are quite good.' Squill puffed out his chest with pride. 'But some animals are extra talented.' Squill's shoulders dropped down in disappointment.

'*Elephants,*' Tally read out from the list. A huge grey animal floated up before her. 'Hmmm, we don't have many of those around here either.'

She continued reading from the list.

'*Bears.*'

Squill drew back nervously as a hologram of a great grizzly bear, black and furry, filled the space in front of them.

Tally's eyes widened as she saw the next creature on the list. Squill waited impatiently for her to read it out:

'*Rats!*'

CHAPTER EIGHT

Tally and Squill stayed up all night in the kitchen. Squill kept guard, checking for signs of Mrs Sneed and Mr Bood, while Tally did the cutting and

bending and

gluing and

sewing and

fixing and

tying

to make the paper bloodhound nose.

By the break of dawn on Sunday, Tally had made a cone-shaped funnel. She strapped it to her face, pointing it out in front of her as if she were wearing a large ice-cream cone. Round the edges were layers of scarves to catch scents. Tally pulled on a big leather ski hat, with long, floppy ear flaps to direct the scent towards the funnel.

'Hooray! It fits!' she cried, taking the nose and hat off again. 'Now we need the sniffing sense.'

Tally and Squill went straight to the stables, picking their way carefully in the dawn light. Tally pushed open the old stable door.

'Brie!' she called. 'Please can you help us?' There was a squeak and the little rat scurried out from behind a pile of logs. Tally put a saucer on the floor. Her mind flitted back to the last time she had asked an animal to share its secret skill – she'd stood right here, with a bowl in her hand, waiting to see if the spiders would give her their special spider essence. She smiled as she remembered how she had used the essence to create a giant cobweb to catch two burglars.

The Molletts had been so relieved. Lord Mollett had even given her his own precious spider brooch as a thank you. This time, it was Brie's sniffing ability she needed.

The book had told Tally the magic words she needed to say:

'Rat, rat,
My heart is true.
Help me learn
To do what you do.'

The second Brie heard the special phrase, she ran to the saucer. She rubbed her pink nose with her teeny paws, as if she was cleaning it. Then into the saucer she put a thin, sparkly liquid. It shone in rainbow colours like oil on water.

'Oh, thank you!' said Tally.

Tally took a tiny paintbrush. Carefully she painted the inside of the funnel. Squill dipped in one furry finger and helped paint the special liquid into the corners.

'Shall we test it?' Tally said, and Squill nodded in excitement.

Tally put on the hat and cone. She fitted the elastic round the back of her head and arranged the scarves into place.

Then she took a deep sniff.

Suddenly the stables smelled stronger! It was a yeasty, straw kind of smell. It slid into the funnel and across the sniffing sense to hit her own nose.

'Wow!' Tally cried. She began to pick out individual scents. There was the deep, spicy smell of wood from the log pile. The sharp scent of the trail Brie had left as she'd run around, smelling a bit like that blue cheese Lord Mollett liked. A soft, musty smell of paper came from the notes in her pinafore pocket, and wafting through the doorway was the fresh scent of grass wet with early morning dew. It was a whole world of new perfumes and odours.

Tally's heart was beating fast. 'Let's find Widdles!' she said.

Floating up from the ground, Tally caught the metallic sniff of an ant nearby,[12] the damp scent of muddy shoes and …

'Yes!'

The heavy, popcorny smell of dog.

'Widdles!' she cried, and she set off on his trail. 'He went this way!'

The scent led all the way to the cliff edge. Here, Tally could smell the scent of twine from the rope ladder, a familiar doggy smell and something else: coconut. It smelled greasy, somehow.

'Colin's hair oil!' Tally shook her head crossly and Squill tutted.

'We have to get Widdles back before the Carriage of Curiosities leaves town today!'

Cautiously, Tally peered over the edge. During the night, the tide had come in and gone out again, and through the misty dawn light she could see huge rocks at the base of the cliff,

[12] The slightly metallic smell of ants comes from formic acid. This acid is found in their bite.

jagged with barnacles. The rope ladder
was swaying in the sea wind,
jumping about against
the side of the cliff. Tally
swallowed hard.

'This doesn't look very
safe, Squill.'
The squirrel nodded in
agreement.

'But we have to find Widdles.'
Squill jumped on to Tally's back and
put his furry paws round her neck.

Tally turned and lay down on her stomach
so the tips of her toes were hanging over
the very edge of the cliff. Slowly, she slid
backwards on the grass, further and
further over the edge. She held tight to the
iron grappling hooks and felt for the first rung
with her toe. There! She put her foot on to the
wooden rung and moved her trembling hands to
the rope. Bit by bit she went down. The first rung,
the second, the third …

The wind swirled around her, bobbing the old ski hat on her head. She was used to rope ladders – she went up and down the one to the Secret Library all the time. But this was different. The library ladder went down inside a shaft in the rock. On it, Tally felt warm and safe, and she knew exactly where the ladder ended. This ladder was in the open air. It swayed from side to side, scraping Tally's knuckles against the side of the cliff. She felt for the next rung and risked a glance down to the rocks – it was a long way! Her heart beat wildly in her ears and her arms began to shake.

'I can't do it, Squill!'

She froze, clinging to the ladder on the cliff edge.

The squirrel chattered softly, stroking her hair until her breath slowed. Tally shut her eyes for a moment. Everyone was depending on her. She had to find Widdles.

Tally gave a deep sniff to calm herself. She smelled salt and seaweed and … wait. What was that? Something else. Something she knew very well. Somewhere nearby was the scent of paper.

Paper and glue and leather. It smelled like a ...
like a book. *How odd!*

Tally shook her head to clear the scent. There
was no time to stop and explore. She tightened her
hands around the rope. On she went. Down and
down. Squill clung tightly to her.

The waves were so rough that a fine spray hit
Tally's legs as she neared the sea. Finally, the soles of
her shoes met hard rock. She was standing on a large
boulder at the base of the cliff. She held tight to the
ladder, ready to pull her feet up if a wave came.

'I don't understand where they went!' Tally called
over the wind. She closed her eyes. She tried to
forget about the wind and the
water and the cold. She
concentrated on the
scent of Widdles.
Tally gave
another deep
sniff. Her
super-nose

picked up dog smell a little way to the right.

Tally opened her eyes. She leaned towards
the doggy scent. Nearby was a mess of seaweed
hanging over an archway.

'Squill. There's something here.' Tally
clambered over to the next rock and parted
the seaweed with her hands. 'Oh, it's a cave. A
hidden sea cave!'

Carefully Tally picked her way into the cave. It
was dark, and the rocks were slimy underfoot.
Water sat in little pools on the cave floor. Tally
turned to look out to sea. She knew about tides.
She'd read all about them in the Secret Library.[13]
Now, the tide was out – the waves were breaking
at the rocks just beyond the cave. But what about
when the tide turned?

'We don't have long, Squill,' she said. 'We
need to search the cave and get out before the tide
starts to come in again.'

She sniffed the air. Her nose caught salt, slime,
damp, earth and then suddenly …

[13] Tides are the rise and fall in sea level. Every day the tide rises to
high tide when the sea is in, and falls to low tide when the sea is out.

Wet dog.

'He was here. Widdles was here!'

Tally frowned, trying to work out what Colin had done next. Did he wait here in the cave for a boat? Did he swim out to sea?

Tally pulled a fat candle and some matches from her pinafore pocket and lit the wick. The light flickered on the cave walls, and disappeared into darkness as the cave stretched back further into the cliff. Tally gave a little shiver.

She climbed over rocks and bumpy stone. At the end of the cave was a narrow tunnel. Tally touched the walls. They had ridges in them, like someone had scraped them, hollowed them out of rock. Suddenly Tally realised something.

'This is a man-made tunnel, Squill! Someone dug out a secret passage in the back of the cave. I wonder where it goes?' She ducked her head beneath the low cave wall and began to follow the tunnel.

The sound of the sea faded until all they could hear was their footsteps and the drip, drip, drip of cave water. Every now and then Tally stopped to check the smells: yes, in between the damp and the slime, there was the dog and the hair oil.

On they went, slipping and sliding through the passage, the candlelight bouncing off the craggy ceiling. Tally held on to the ragged stone walls to keep her balance. Squill clung on tight to her neck.

Then, just when Tally was beginning to think the tunnel would never end, she saw shafts of sunlight ahead of her.

'Squill! We're nearly out!'

Together they ran to the light. Thick strands of ivy hung down like a doorway, rays of sun flickering in between the leaves. Tally pushed the trailing stems aside and stepped out, soft grass beneath her feet. They were in a field at the end of the village.

Tally gave a huge sniff. She caught the scent of sawdust and the earthy smell of animals – not just one dog, lots of animals.

'He went this way!' She led the way over to the side of the field towards a group of trees. Sniffing all the time, Tally parted the branches of the trees and there in front of her was the large wooden wagon, with small carriages lined up behind it. The Carriage of Curiosities!

'I knew it,' Tally whispered. Squill squeaked in answer.

She pulled off her hat and sniffing nose, and folded them into her pinafore pocket for safety.

'Widdles! Widdles!' she called. There was an answering bark.

Tally ran all the way along the carriages, following the barking.

At the end of the line was a low carriage with a wire lid. Inside was Widdles! The puppy yapped to see Tally. She knelt down to open the catch and lift him out on to the grass. He wriggled in happiness, licking her face, her arms, her hands, even her elbows.

Just then there was a rustling noise behind her, a noise that sent Squill diving into Tally's pinafore pocket for safety.

Rough hands yanked up Tally.

'I thought I'd just get the dog,' a snarling voice said, 'but now I'll take that squirrel too.'

'Let us go!' Tally wriggled and kicked.

Widdles tried to bite Colin's leg, but – at the last moment – he got distracted by a leaf and chewed that instead.

'You can go – if you give me the dog,' said Colin, 'and the squirrel as well. He'd be perfect in my show.'

'No!' shouted Tally. 'Never!'

Squill burrowed down further, hiding at the bottom of her pocket.

'Then there's only one thing for it,' Colin growled. He lifted her off her feet and shoved her into the big wagon. Then he threw Widdles in after her and locked the door.

They were trapped!

CHAPTER NINE

Tally rattled the door.

'Let us go!' she shouted.

She ran to the bars on the window and shook them as hard as she could, but they held fast.

'Squill, see if you can fit between them!'

Squill sucked his tummy in and tried, but he couldn't squeeze through.

'Oh, what should we do?' Tally sank to the floor. Tears trickled down her cheeks. Widdles climbed on to her lap to lick them off.

Colin moved up and down outside the wagon, bossing the animals and locking the cages ready for departure. Soon they would be leaving! It was no good crying. She had to do something.

Tally stood up. 'I'm going to get us out of here –
all of us.'

She blinked away the last of her tears and looked
around the room. It was small in here, like a wooden
corridor. There was just enough space to hold a
narrow bench and a table. At the end was a wide
shelf covered in cushions – that must be where Colin
slept. The walls were covered in shelves holding bags
of sawdust, animal feed, rugs, whips and costumes.

Tally lifted her eyes to the ceiling, thinking hard.
Oh – there was a hatch! A narrow hatch in the roof
to let in air. It was too high above her to reach. She
looked around for something to stand on, but the
table and bench were nailed down tight to stop them
moving when the wagon travelled.

Tally could hear Colin outside.

'Right you lot,' he snapped. 'Get your costumes
on! I don't want any of your old owners recognising
you as we pass by.'

Tally burned with anger. She was right! Colin was
stealing animals. She glanced at the posters on his
table, ready to be put up in the next village.

COME TO COLIN'S CARRIAGE OF CURIOSITIES!

MARVEL AT THE DANCING GECKO!

APPLAUD THE BICYCLING BUDGIE!

GASP AT THE FIRE-BREATHING CAT!

SIGH WHEN THE GUINEA PIG SINGS!

ALL THIS PLUS

JUGGLING HAMSTERS, CLOWNING BEES,

ACROBATIC RABBITS AND MORE!

LOOK OUT FOR THE CARRIAGE

MOVING THROUGH YOUR VILLAGE.

That cat ... it looked familiar ...

Where have I seen it before?

'It's Mrs Marsh's missing cat!' Tally pointed at the poster. 'Look, it has one black ear, one white. Here's Mr Nibbles the guinea pig too, with his white tummy.'

Tally marched back and forth under the hatch. 'Colin is going from village to village, stealing animals and training them up before moving on.

We have to get out of here and rescue them.'

She looked up at the hatch. An idea was forming. But first ... first she had to distract Colin.

Tally pulled out her hat and sniffing nose.

'There must be something useful in this wagon,' she said, 'and I'm going to smell it out.'

She put the nose in place and gave a deep sniff. She smelled wood, damp and musty. She smelled straw and sawdust and ... a sweet, cloying smell ... What was that? It smelled sugary and earthy ... like ...

'Oh!' cried Tally. 'It's the bees! The Mollett Manor bees!'

She ran towards the scent. There on the sideboard was a wooden box. It had little holes poked in the lid. From the box came the sound of buzzing.

Tally peered out of the window. Colin was busy hitching up the wagon.

'I wonder,' she said, and Squill pricked up his ears. Tally continued, 'Do you remember we read that bees can recognise faces?'

Squill nodded.

'Shall we test that theory?'

Tally held the corner of the box, ready to open the lid. Her heart was beating fast – what if the bees stung her?

She held the box right by the window and slowly prised open the lid. Hundreds of bees flew out. Each was dressed in a little clown costume, with a brightly coloured curly wig and big boots on all six feet. For a moment the cloud of bees turned towards Tally. She held her breath and pointed a trembling finger in the direction of Colin.

There was a buzz of recognition. Then the colony flew straight out of the window towards the man they remembered stealing them from their home.

'Eeeeee!' squealed Colin as the angry cloud surrounded him. He raced across the field.

'Buzz! Buzz!' The bees chased him in and out of the trees.

'Now for the second part of the plan,' said
Tally. 'Come on, Widdles.' She lifted him on
to her shoulders. 'Stand up on your hind legs –
that's right.' He balanced in place. 'Now, Squill.
Climb up and stand on Widdles.'

Paw over paw, the red squirrel made his way
up Tally and then up Widdles. They
formed a wobbly, furry tower.

'Can you reach the hatch?' Tally
called from the floor.

Squill stood on his tiptoes,
his feet on the puppy's head.
He stretched until his claws
reached the hatch. He
pulled himself up and …
he was out!

'Get the keys!' Tally
called to him as she kept
an eye on Colin. The silly
man was still running
from the bees. 'They're on
Colin's belt.'

Squill crouched behind a wheel of the wagon.
The next time Colin ran squealing by, he held
out his paw and …

snatch!

He yanked off the keys.

Quick as a flash, Squill clambered up the steps
of the carriage and slid the key into the brass
lock, his paws scratching against the metal. Tally
heard a click and heaved her body against the
door. She and Widdles tumbled out.

'Ahhhh!' yelled Colin, still running round in
circles.

'Quick, get inside!' Tally called to him, pushing
the door wider. 'It's the only safe place.'

Colin dashed past her, straight through the
open wagon door. Tally shut the door behind him
and turned the key. The thief was trapped!

Tally strolled down the line of carriages,
opening cage after cage. She let out the rabbits,
and the ants, and the hamsters, and the budgie,
and the gecko, and Mrs Marsh's cat.

He gave a 'Meow!' and ran off home.

Finally there was only one cage left to open.

'Mr Nibbles?' Tally asked, and the little guinea pig nodded. 'Let's get you out,' said Tally gently. She unlocked his cage and lifted him up. He snuggled into her hand and nibbled her fingers gratefully. 'There you go.' Tally put him in her pinafore pocket. 'We'll take him to the cottage with the blue door,' she said. 'Adam will be so happy.'

She looked around at the rest of the animals. Who knew which village they had come from? How could she ever get them home? Tally did the next best thing.

'If anyone wants to come with me,' she called out in a clear voice, 'I can give you a home somewhere warm, with lots of food and water and company.'

A procession moved across the village green.

There was a girl,

a squirrel,

a dog,

a budgie,

a gecko,

three hamsters,

four rabbits,

one hundred ants,

and a cloud of bees.

First they went to the police. Tally handed over
the brass key to the carriage.

'You might want to pay a visit to Colin's
Carriage of Curiosities,' she told the officer. 'Ask
him where he gets his animals from.'

Then they knocked at the cottage with the blue
door.

'Hello?' Adam opened the door, wearing his
pyjamas. He squealed with delight when he saw
the guinea pig sitting in Tally's open palms.

'Mr Nibbles!' he cried. 'You've
come home! Thank you.' He
gave Tally a fierce hug, until
Mr Nibbles squealed to stop
himself from being crushed
between their bodies.

Tally smiled at Adam. 'I'm glad Mr Nibbles is safe now.' Then she waved goodbye and led her long line of animals through the village, down the path and into the manor grounds.

The bees buzzed gratefully and flew straight home to their hives. Tally headed for the stables.

'Brie?' she called as she opened the stable door. There was an answering squeak. 'I've brought a few friends for you.'

Brie's little pink nose emerged from a pile of straw. The black rabbits hopped over to her. The gecko jumped onto the wall and found the dampest corner of the building to hide in. The hamsters went to sleep in the hay. The budgie flew up to the rafters, and the ants explored the floor.

Tally smiled. Every animal was happy.

The village clock chimed seven.

'Quick, Squill! We've only four hours till the party!' She'd nearly forgotten all about the most important event in Lady Beatrice's calendar.

With Widdles in her arms, she ran into the manor house and up the stairs to the blue drawing room. Light came from under the crack in the doorway.

Tally burst into the room.

'I've found Widdles!' she cried.

CHAPTER TEN

'Oh! Oh!' Lady Beatrice sat up from where she lay on the sofa. 'Lord William!' she cried. 'Mama's little baby! I'm so glad you're all right!' She scooped Widdles into her arms and covered him in kisses. Widdles barked in delight and chewed the ribbon on her hat.

Once Lady Beatrice had been reunited with her favourite dog in the whole world, the manor became a hive of activity. The next four hours passed in a frantic whirl of cake-baking, flower-arranging, cleaning, polishing and scrubbing.

Mrs Sneed swept the cobblestones (grumbling all the time).

Mr Bood mowed the lawn into a spiral pattern (then sneakily had a little nap in the middle of the swirl).

Lady Beatrice cut up cucumber sandwiches in the kitchen. ('Isn't this fun, Tally! I never even knew we had a kitchen. You must have a lovely time down here baking and eating.')

And Lord Mollett hung bunting from every tree of the garden.

Tally's job was to make a cake. The bees allowed her to take a huge honeycomb from their hive, dripping with soft yellow honey. She fired up the huge old bread oven in the kitchen, used by the monks hundreds of years ago. Then she got out the largest mixing bowl.

She and Squill made a ginormous honey cake, with seventeen layers, dusted in cinnamon-sugar. On top they added teeny bees made out of yellow fondant icing, with black liquorice stripes.

By mid-morning everything was ready.

Lord Mollett and Lady Beatrice unlocked the gate at Mollett Manor and, for the first time in eleven years, guests poured in. They came from all over the village. The schoolmistress was there, and the postman and the doctor and little Adam and Mrs Marsh (with her cat). Some came from further afield, old friends of Lord Mollett and Lady Beatrice's – dukes and duchesses and knights and dames and barons and baronesses.

Lady Beatrice was wearing her fanciest hat. It had lace and ribbons and feathers and glitter – and bits of cucumber that had accidentally fallen on it earlier. Lord Mollett wore a dusty old top hat and a moth-eaten jacket. They stood side by side, welcoming everyone with a smile.

'We did it, Squill,' Tally whispered as she watched the guests eating the lovely honey cake. She waved at Adam, she patted Mrs Marsh's cat and she saved Widdles from falling in a puddle. There was a flash of movement and she looked down to see Brie leading a long line of hamsters, rabbits and ants scampering under tables to nibble cake crumbs. The budgie chattered from a branch above her, and Tally hugged her arms around herself. Everyone was happy. Tally felt a bubble of joy swell up inside her. She had done all this. The girl who slept in a sink had made all this happen.

'Ma would be proud,' she said.

Squill solemnly chewed the end of her ponytail.

She sensed someone beside her. It was Lord Mollett.

'Good job, Tally,' he said. 'Thank you.' He opened his hand. There on his palm was a round golden pendant. 'I want you to have this.'

'But … but that's your family heirloom!' Tally spluttered.

'You don't understand how much you've helped us by finding William.' He looked towards Lady Beatrice, who was bending down to kiss the puppy. Widdles was licking the slices of cucumber off her hat.

'My sister is a very delicate sort of person,'

Lord Mollett explained. 'It's my fault. I did something, years ago … There was a scandal and it affected Beatrice dreadfully.' He hung his head. 'She was engaged, you see, but I spoiled everything for her. For the last eleven years she's been hiding herself away here at the manor. No more parties, no more friends, no more suitors. And now look at her!' He smiled as Beatrice chatted to her guests, Widdles in her arms.

Lord Mollett turned back to Tally. 'You and Beatrice are all the family I have.' Tally knew how he felt. 'So, please – I'd like to give the pendant to you.'

'Thank you,' she said. 'I would be honoured.' She grinned till her cheeks hurt.

Of course, Tally had to clear up after the party. But she didn't mind. All the animals helped her, carrying cups and plates in their paws and teeth. Even Widdles tried to help by picking up spoons and burying them in the garden.

All Lord Mollett's talk of family had made Tally feel restless. When the last glass had been cleared away, she walked out to the cliffs and stood at the safety rope, gazing across the sea. Would she ever find out what had happened to her mother?

'I'm happy, Ma,' she whispered across the pounding waves. 'But I wish you were here.'

She glanced down. The iron grapples were still there. She'd have to pull them out so no one else could get on to the manor grounds, but … first … there was something tugging at her mind … something out of place, something she had to sort out.

She frowned. All at once, she remembered.

'Paper!'

Squill raised his eyebrows.

'I smelled paper when I climbed down the ladder. Paper and leather and glue, like there was a book down there.'

A vague memory crept into her head. Ma, on the day she'd fallen, eight years ago. She'd been reaching for something at the edge of the cliff.

'Stay here, Widdles!' Tally tied him to a tree to make sure he didn't follow her. Then she pulled on her sniffing nose. All of a sudden the sharp smell of salt and seaweed filled her nostrils.

Squill chattered in excitement and jumped on to her back. Tally carefully felt her way down three rungs of the rope ladder and stopped.

'It was around here that I smelled it,' she said. She gave a deep sniff – yes, there it was again. Paper and leather and glue.

She held on to the ladder tightly with one hand, while the other felt for niches or gaps in the rocky face of the cliff. She pulled a rock away from the cliff and behind it was a hole!

Tally thrust her hand inside and her fingers touched something. She drew it out. It was a book. A little leather-bound book. How long had it been hidden here? What stories did it contain? And what connection did it have to Ma? Clutching it tightly, Tally climbed back up to solid ground.

She pulled off her sniffing nose, and with shaking fingers, she opened the cover.

Martha's Diary

'Dear diary,' Tally read out loud. 'Today is my seventeenth birthday ...'

Tally's eyes widened. She recognised the writing. It was handwriting she had seen once before, in the margin of a book in the library.

'It's Ma's writing!' she told Squill. 'Ma's diary!' Her heart was pounding in her chest. So this was what Ma had reached for, the day she

disappeared. 'Martha,' Tally whispered. It was the first time she could remember hearing her mother's name.

Tally turned to the cliff edge. The wind was howling now and she could hear the waves crashing below. Ma had fallen off that cliff, and she'd never been seen again.

'She's dead,' Mrs Sneed often reminded Tally with a hint of glee. But Tally never thought of her as dead, just missing.

And now a chain of thought began to form in Tally's head. What if it was high tide when Ma fell?

Maybe Ma had landed in the water at the bottom of the cliff.

Maybe she'd been stuck there, floating, with no way to get back up.

Maybe she'd floated for hours and hours.

Then … when the tide went out …

Tally frowned and Squill patted her shoulder to encourage her.

Maybe Ma had spotted the sea cave.

Crawled along the tunnel.

But that would mean …

'What if she really isn't dead?' The words were out of Tally's mouth before she could stop them. Dangerous words. Words full of hope.

Squill watched Tally's face carefully. She felt her eyes filling with tears as she held the diary close. A thought hit her. The last time she'd read Martha's handwriting in the library, she'd seen a hologram of Ma. The image of Martha as a young girl had floated up out of the book.

Hope built in Tally's heart. If she took the diary inside to the library and read it there, would she … might she …

'Could I see Ma?'

CHAPTER ELEVEN

Tally's hands were shaking as she climbed down into the library below. It took her three tries before she could get the lamps lit. Her trembling fingers kept dropping the matches. Finally she struck a light and the soft lamp glow sent yellow light across the thousands of shelves. The spines of the books sparkled and glittered, calling to her to open them. But there was only one book Tally wanted.

Squill had sensed the solemn mood. He marched in a straight line before Tally, his tail held rigid behind him. He flicked the blanket to iron out the wrinkles and smoothed it down for Tally.

She sat down and put the diary between them. She stroked its leather cover, her fingers longing to touch anywhere Ma might have touched.

'There might be some answers in here,' she said softly. 'About Ma and why she brought me here. Here goes …' she said. Her heart was beating wildly.

She turned the page.

'Dear diary, today is my seventeenth birthday ...'

As Tally read, an image appeared, floating up in the air before her. It was of a lady with curly hair and green eyes.

'Ma!' Tally whispered. She grinned so widely her cheeks hurt. It worked! The magic of the Secret Library had worked! Here was Ma.

Her mother was older than she'd been in the first hologram, when she was a young girl, working in the library. The hologram before Tally now was of a woman. Her hair was darker. Her long dress was frilly, and the sleeves were enormous puffy things. Tally couldn't imagine

climbing trees in that dress, or climbing through
the trapdoor into the library. She breathed in –
Ma smelled of lavender. She was sitting at a desk
in a bedroom. It wasn't anywhere in Mollett
Manor. The wallpaper behind her had birds on,
and the window looked out on to a garden.

Ma's face was glowing with happiness. Her
cheeks were flushed pink as she wrote.

'The sun came out just in time for our picnic.'

All at once the hologram switched to show a
picnic rug spread out by a lake. Tally
frowned. She peered closer. The
lake had a willow tree that
was very familiar …

Tally gasped. 'That's
the tree at Mollett
Manor! Ma came to
the manor house
for a picnic on her
birthday!'

Tally was so
excited she

dropped the book and the hologram disappeared.

With trembling fingers she picked up Ma's diary and found her place.

'Bear looked dashing as usual.' Tally continued reading out loud what Ma had written. 'I saw him walking over towards me and my heart felt like it would burst with joy.'

Bear.

The world stilled for a moment.

Bear was Ma's character, the one she spoke about all the time.

'Bear is a person,' she whispered in awe.

A hologram man walked through the trees towards the picnic rug. The sun was warm, and a breeze lifted from the pages of the book to blow Tally's curls around her face.

The man wore a suit and a top hat. On his arm was a picnic basket, on his face was a broad smile and on his jacket was a spider brooch.

Suddenly Tally recognised him.

'Oh!' she cried out. The book fell closed on her lap and the hologram man disappeared.

'Squill! Did you see?' Her voice was shaking.

The red squirrel nodded. His little paws were trembling, and he brushed his tail over and over again.

'It was Lord Mollett,' Tally breathed, 'Lord Edward Mollett. Teddy is short for Edward ... Teddy ... Bear.'

Tally stared at Squill. 'Lord Mollett is Ma's Bear.'

Tally pictured Lord Mollett, leaning over to help her with her sums, laughing at a joke she'd made. Lord Mollett, who thought she was clever and wise. Lord Mollett who had given Tally that very spider brooch.

'Someone special made it for me,' he'd said.

Climbing to her feet, she pulled the golden pendant out of her pocket and turned it over and over. One thought would not leave her head. A thought so shocking she was almost afraid to say it out loud.

She carefully folded up the blanket. Holding it to her chest, she gazed around the Secret Library, lit golden by the lamps. This was the place her mum had come to time and again, the same place she'd brought Tally. A place of magic. But now, she realised that Mollett Manor had meant more than magic to her mother – it had meant love.

Her mind whirling, Tally carried her friend over to the ladder leading out of the Secret Library. She climbed back up the ladder and emerged in the circle of stones. Beyond them stood the house where Tally the servant girl slept in the sink.

'Squill,' she whispered. Her voice was shaking. 'Do you think Lord Mollett is my father?'

Squill placed his paw in her hand and gave it a squeeze.

Then, together, the two of them began to walk back towards the kitchen.

It was time to peel the potatoes.

Acknowledgements

My thanks go to Eve White – who has supported
me right from the start; Lena, Karen and Becca
for all their help kicking the story into shape;
and to James Brown for his fantastic illustrations.
Also to the Scattered Authors' Society – I *could* do
it without you, but it would be a lot less fun. —
Abie Longstaff

Huge thanks once again to the marvellously
creative Sophie Burdess at Little, Brown who
allows me free rein (and plenty of illustration
space!). Appreciation too goes to Emily Talbot
and Molly Jamieson at United Agents. Most of
all, thank you to Abie who draws me maps and
has created this wonderful step back in time for
us to explore and immerse ourselves in. (Also,
thanks to Hazel, our guinea pig, who posed
beautifully.) — James Brown

ABOUT THE AUTHOR

ABIE LONGSTAFF is the eldest of six children and grew up in Australia, Hong Kong and France. She knows all about squabbling and bossing younger sisters around so she began her career as a barrister. She started writing when her children were born. Her books include *The Fairytale Hairdresser* series and *The Magic Potions Shop* books. She has a life-long love of fairy tales and mythology, and her work is greatly influenced by these themes.

Abie got the idea for *The Trapdoor Mysteries* from her parents' house in France. The house is big and old, with lots of rooms and outbuildings. In one of the bedrooms, there is a secret entrance hidden in a fireplace. It leads to a room that was used by the French Resistance during the war. It was the perfect idea for a book!

Abie lives with her family by the seaside in Hove.

ABOUT THE ILLUSTRATOR

Inspired by a school visit from Anthony Browne at the age of eight, JAMES BROWN has wanted to illustrate ever since. Having won the SCBWI's Undiscovered Voices 2014 competition, he had illustrated the *Elspeth Hart* series and two of his own *Archie and George* books. Two picture books he has written, *With My Mummy* and *With My Daddy*, are recently out and his first author-illustrator picture book is released for Christmas 2018. He is the illustrator for the new *Al's Awesome Science* series. James comes from Nottingham and has two cheeky daughters who usually take off with his favourite crayons.

FIND OUT WHAT HAPPENS IN
TALLY AND SQUILL'S NEXT ADVENTURE . . .

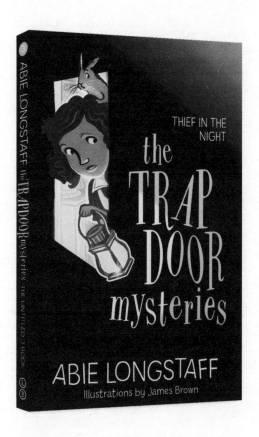